Ollie's Cabin in the Woods

To Scott Owens

Thanks for your interest in THE "Irmstead"

Bob Armstrong

Oliver Johnson

Ollie's Cabin in the Woods

Robert and Katheryn Hessong

Illustrations by
Carolyn Hessong Hickman

Guild Press of Indiana, Inc.

GUILD PRESS OF INDIANA, INC.
435 Gradle Drive
Carmel, Indiana 46032
317-848-6421

ISBN 1-57860-031-6 (PAPERBACK)
ISBN 1-57860-045-6 (HARDCOVER)

Library of Congress
Catalog Card Number
99-99734

Text designed by Sheila G. Samson

Printed and bound in the United States of America

Contents

Remembering the Past

This book is about the real pioneer life of an early Hoosier, Oliver Johnson, and his family.

Oliver — or Ollie, as he was called — told the stories of his growing-up years to his grandson, who wrote them down on a plain school tablet at the beginning of the twentieth century. Then the tablet was put away in a chest for almost fifty years. However, Ollie's grandson told the stories to his own young grandson and granddaughter in the 1940s.

Those children, Oliver Johnson's great-great-grand-children, are Robert Hessong, one of the authors, and Carolyn Hessong Hickman, the illustrator of this book. Robert and Carolyn spent much of their childhood hearing of Grandpa Oliver's ways and even living among his furnishings, which their grandfather and parents had inherited. They decided to rewrite their great-great-grand-father's stories for children today. Robert's wife, Katheryn, an elementary school teacher, helped with the project, and so young readers are given a glimpse of how life was lived in early Indiana around 1840.

In truth, we all have stories to share with those who

are born after us. Ollie wasn't a president, a general, or a known inventor. He was a just an ordinary man who worked with his hands, embraced and joyously loved his family, and created an atmosphere for listening to one another.

We hope you enjoy the tales of Ollie's cabin in the woods, and learning about pioneer ways!

Robert and Katheryn Hessong
and Carolyn Hessong Hickman
August 1999

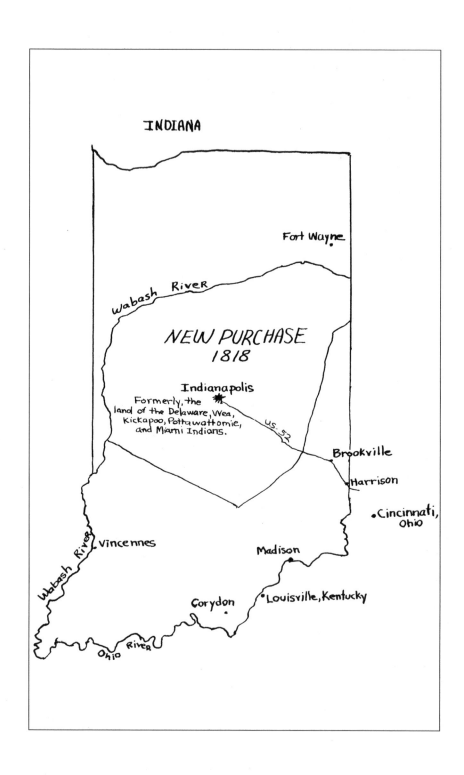

From Virginia to the Indiana Woodland

My Ancestors

My name is Oliver Johnson, and I want to share my memories with you. Before I was born in 1821, my father, my grandfather, and my uncles walked from their home near Brookville, Indiana, to a place called the New Purchase. This recently opened land was in the same county that eventually became Indianapolis.

My grandparents were real pioneers when they came to the Indiana Territory in the late 1700s. Jeremiah Johnson, my grandfather, was born in Virginia near the time of the Revolutionary War. Since his blacksmithing skills were needed, as families migrated west after the war, he came with his wife, Jane Lawson Johnson, and their children to Kentucky. My father, John Johnson, was born in the new place.

Jane, my grandmother, had been given two slaves by her Southern parents when their plantation was sold. But before the Johnsons moved to new lands in Kentucky, they chose to free the slaves.

When the Indiana Territory opened in 1800, the Johnsons proceeded on and purchased land in Franklin County, Indiana, northwest of Cincinnati, Ohio. Moving on to new challenges was part of this family's character.

Grandfather's preaching, farming, and his money-making trade of blacksmithing provided his family with a good life. Blacksmiths were very important citizens who provided all of the metal needs of the pioneers. These included hinges, fences, horseshoes, wagon parts, eating utensils, fireplace tools, and farm implements. All of these useful items helped make life bearable in this primitive and remote area. The path near Grandpap's cabin was named Johnson Fork Road, because everyone knew how important he was to the community.

John Johnson, my father, was born in Kentucky in 1798. Pap, as I called him, grew up in the rolling hill land of the southeastern corner of the Indiana Territory. He, too, learned blacksmithing and farming from his father.

Pap married my mother, Sarah Pursel, around 1818 and moved a short distance away to Harrison, Indiana, which was named for the well-known Harrison family of political fame. William Henry Harrison had been an Indian fighter and served as governor of the Northwest Territory until 1812. He was elected President of the United States in 1841. His grandson, Benjamin Harrison, became President of the United States in 1889.

Pap Buys Land in the New Purchase

By 1816 the Indiana Territory had enough residents to qualify for statehood. So Corydon, near the Ohio River, was chosen to be the capital of the new state.

When the Delaware, Kickapoo, Miami, Potawatomi, and Wea Indians were removed from the Indiana Territory in the center of the new state, the lands there were offered for sale by the U.S. government. This newly opened, tree-covered land was called the New Purchase. The rich soil was greatly desired by the farmers. So when my Grandfather Jeremiah learned that a land-sale office was opening in Brookville, he looked ahead and decided to help his children, who were now young adults.

Blacksmithing money provided new homesteads in this area for most of Grandpap's children. Jeremiah purchased several eighty-acre parcels of land for $1.25 per acre. These plots were given to Jeremiah and Jane's children. Each son or daughter was given a land grant from the U.S. government and signed by President James Monroe. This paper meant that each family was the first owner of their eighty acres.

By the time Pap got to his land on Fall Creek, six other cabins were already in the vicinity. Grandpap bought farms nearby for Pap's brothers, Jerry and Tom, so they could help one another with the challenges of breaking the new land.

Pap, Uncle Jerry, Uncle Tom, and Grandfather Jeremiah went to see their purchase in the late spring of 1821. They felled trees, built a simple cabin, cleared land, planted corn, and prepared to bring their families to the new home. Pap had left his wife, Sarah, and young daughter, Louisa, back in Harrison for this "men only" worktime. The womenfolk needed to keep their gardens tended, and food needed to be preserved for the long winter ahead.

Harvesting the first crop of corn on the new land up northwest had taken until late November. When the men returned to the Whitewater area in the late fall, they were pleased to know a son had been born to Sarah and John.

My birthday — November 21, 1821 — had passed before their return, with women attending the birthing of the baby with the father far away. I was named Oliver, and I was Pap and Mother's first son. Now little Louisa, their first child, had a brother.

The rest of the winter was spent planning for our complete move to the new farm.

The Trip to Our New Homestead

Later in the spring of 1822, my family loaded our ox cart with the most useful items, including tools made by Grandpap. With an infant and a young daughter to tend to, the packing and loading was carefully planned. The breaking plow, which would be used to break the new soil, was one of the most important tools to be loaded.

Mother sat on a seat in the cart holding me and clutching small Louisa close beside her. Pap walked beside the oxen-pulled cart. He managed to direct the oxen and herd along our milk cow, some chickens, and our pigs. These animals trailed the cart. Of course, our relatives and their animals and goods followed us along the rutted path.

We needed ten traveling days to get to the new farmstead. At night we could camp out and sleep under the ox cart. Country taverns or inns also gave us better rest for a few nights. The animals foraged on grasses, berries, and insects along the way. Creeks were plentiful on this route to the New Purchase, so our water supply was always nearby. [Likely this pathway was somewhat parallel to State Road 52 that transverses Indiana today.]

The slow movement of the oxen no doubt made the trip seem very long. At last we came to the three-acre clearing and our new cabin which had hastily been built on the western banks of Fall Creek. Large trees surrounded our small cabin and Pap's cleared land.

The men had chosen the high rise of the earth above Fall Creek to erect the cabin. Settling in didn't take long.

Building a Cabin in the Woods

Digging the Well

Pap got busy finding an elm pole to use so he could dig our well for water. He used this elm pole for a sweep that he attached to a crotched tree located at the site of the future waterhole. On the end of the elm pole he fastened a rope tied to a wooden bucket brought from our former home. This apparatus would serve to lift the water out of the well after it was dug. For now Pap could use it to lift the dirt out as he dug the well. The water level in this place was only eighteen to twenty feet deep. After much dirt had been removed from the hole, his shovel hit a clean gravel bed with water. He built a three feet high box from puncheons, which were shaved slices of a tree. This box needed to fit around the top of the open well. I got many a good drink from that place!

The year's corn crop had to be planted as soon as the earth warmed from winter. Again the almost three acres would have to feed our family and animals that next season. So as soon as the well was done, it was planting time.

WELL
SWEEP

Neighbors Help Build Our Barn

With the season of winter ahead, Pap knew the barn had to be built next. Our oxen, chickens, pigs, and milk cow provided us with either workpower or food. Thus a warm shelter from the unknown winters here was a necessity.

To begin with, Pap and his brothers, who were starting their own farms in the New Purchase area near our farm, gathered in some large logs to frame the barn.

After the foundation logs were put into place, a barn-raising was called. At this time all of the neighbors came and the men put the barn together while the women brought their special dishes of food for the feast that was a part of these special days. Some of the children helped with the project while younger ones played and enjoyed themselves.

At times women and girls brought dishes for which they were famous or with which they hoped to secure a community reputation. Cooperative enterprises such as this barn raising were popular and needed among the

pioneers; and they might also include log cabin raising, harvesting, and hog butchering for the men, as well as quiltings and apple parings for the women. These times, as I grew older, were some of the most memorable occasions of my youth. It was important that you took the time to help your neighbors after they had been generous with their time to help you.

Pap Clears More Land

All around us were endless trees. The forest was a problem for pioneers who needed to cultivate the land for food. With a growing family, Pap needed more than the three acres he cleared last year. He first cut trees that were small such as eighteen inches or less in diameter. After the trees were felled, the smaller trees were dragged and stacked against the larger trees. Oxen pulled bushes and grubs out by their roots. All of these unusable forest parts were  fired and burned. As the trees burned, we had to continue to readjust the burning timbers and bushes so that all were turned to ash. Eyes of the pioneers stung from the constant wood smoke. Pap's objective was to get rid of as many trees as possible in a short time. The Johnson family's food supply of corn needed to be planted.

Larger trees had to wait until the third year of Pap's ownership of the land. The largest trees were girdled when he had time before crop harvest. To girdle a tree, he used his adz to chop out the bark and make a ring around the oak, poplar, or ash trees. This injury to the tree would stop the flow of food to the leaves from the soil, and the tree would die. A dry, lifeless tree is easier to cut.

Pap Builds a Cabin Loft

Shortly after my first birthday, winter came. Pap's second harvest of corn was done, and he knew it was time to enlarge the eighteen-by-twenty-foot cabin. Since pioneer families had many children, he wanted to be ready.

Building a sleeping loft in the space overhead was a task for the cold season. Pap placed wood planks on the crossbeams of the cabin. These crossbeams rest on the top logs of the cabin's side walls. When the planks were in

tightly the room now had a flat ceiling over half of it. Steps to reach the loft were carved into a poplar log that had a diameter of two feet. This ladder was placed against a wall, and Pap added rails so that climbing into the loft was safer.

As I grew older, I slept in this warm loft with my brothers: Luther, Volney, and Newton. Always we were so tired by the time we crawled up to the loft, sleep came immediately. Since the fireplace heat rises, this place was very warm and comfortable.

Cabin Raising for a Neighbor

Since I was a baby when my family came to the new land, I was not a worker for raising our family's cabin. However, by the time I was eight or so, I did help make either a lean-to house for pioneers in a hurry, a squared-beam cabin, or a whole tree-log cabin.

When pioneers got to their new land in late summer or fall, they had to cut small logs for a three-sided shelter called a lean-to. They would cut  smaller trees and place them on three sides of the home. The open side had a fire pit in front. This helped keep the tired folks warm and also protect them from the wild animals.

As new land owners came to their forested acres, Pap was asked to come help raise their cabin. By the time I was eight, I went with him.

Most settlers had spent weeks cutting log-sized trees before they sent word to nearby neighbors to come and raise a cabin. By the time Pap and I brought our tools and oxen to help, the pioneer farmer had pulled all of the needed logs up to the cabin site with his oxen.

Now the big day was here! Sounds of voices and tromping animals pulling wagons could be heard through the woods. Settlers I hadn't even met yet came to volunteer their talents. Helping a neighbor bound us together forever.

The strongest men placed a large rock on each of the four corners of the cabin base after the ground had been leveled off. The four best ax men were placed in each corner to make saddles and notches for the logs to lay firmly in place. An ox team would drag the twelve-inch-in-diameter logs to the exact spot where they were needed.

Two side logs were flattened a little on the bottom and placed on the rocks. These made a stable base for the logs piled on top. I watched the ax men very closely as they made the notches. I was fascinated at how they cut them so accurately and made them fit firmly in the corners.

This process of cutting and fitting logs in place went on until the men could no longer lift the logs in place. Logs were then rolled up an inclined plane by men who pulled

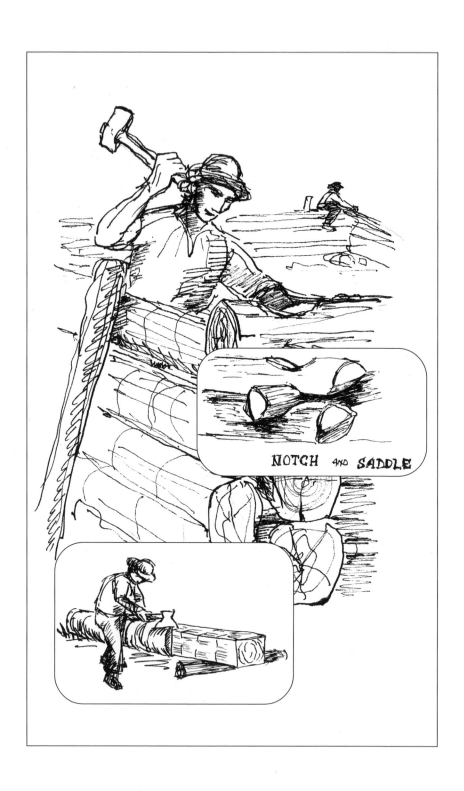

NOTCH AND SADDLE

them with ropes while others pushed. This ramp was made from two poles. When I saw all four sides of the cabin in place, I knew that the neighbors would soon have a cabin.

By this time the men surely needed the many drinks of water that I had carried from the nearest neighbor's well or a flowing spring. I always felt proud when I could help end a worker's thirst.

When the four walls of logs were about a foot higher than a man's head, it was time to build the roof. A very straight log was laid as a foundation for the roof on each of the two lengths or sides of the cabin. I watched as men cut the end or gable logs different lengths. Great care was given to making certain that the angle of the roof would shed melting snow. The logs were notched and fit carefully.

Preparing the clapboard shingles had been done all morning by talented men who brought the special tools. The roof itself was made of clapboards which were split from straight-grained oak cuts, three or four feet long. A special tool called a froe was used to cut the clapboards. These roofing boards were cut from a piece of oak wood six or eight inches wide and half to three quarters of an inch thick. They were laid in rows across the roof logs. A second row of clapboards was laid over the first row to cover the cracks, and then the next row of clapboards overlapped the row below. These boards were tied down by weight poles. The poles were in turn notched into the gable logs at either end to prevent them from sliding down. No nails were used. Later when pioneers had more time and blacksmiths were available, nails would be used. Sometimes, as I slept in the loft, snow would blow in between the cracks in the clapboards, but I just pulled my head in under the covers and went to sleep.

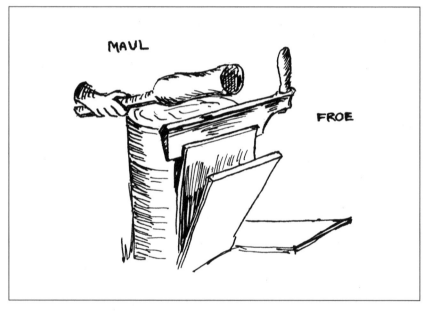

After the four walls of the cabin were up and the roof was on tightly, the doors, windows, and fireplace holes were cut out. On this cabin we cut two doors, one on each side of the cabin. Often the family horse would drag a big log in for the fireplace—going in one door and out the other. One or two window holes would be cut out at this time, and, if available, some imported glass would be installed; but often only a thin skin or some greased paper

would have to suffice. These early windows made the inside of the cabin uncomfortable in cold weather. The chill of the cold came through every opening.

Pioneers learned quickly that a floor was essential for Indiana winters. The men cut small trees and put these logs, called joists, eighteen inches apart across the cabin from one wall to another. Then the men made two- to three-inch-thick split boards of grained oak or ash. An adz was then used to shave down the puncheons, as the floor boards were called. Even though pioneer children had thick calloused feet, they still got splinters in their feet from the rough floors.

I watched as one man, an excellent carpenter, made the door. It was made from puncheons pinned together and hung on wooden hinges made of a block of wood and a pin. The latch was a big wooden bar fastened at one end across the inside of the door. A slot was made for the latch to drop into in order to hold the door fast.

A hole was bored through the door just above the latch, and a latch string made from deer hide was installed. Most people kept the latch string on the inside of the house. When the owners were sure they knew who was knocking, then the latch string was pushed through the hole toward the visitor. The guest would then pull it upward for easy entry.

In order to make a quick-drawing fireplace, the builder had to make very correct measurements. So I watched and listened very carefully. Someday I would need to use this skill.

At one end of the cabin, an opening eight feet wide and five feet high was cut out for the fireplace. The hearth for the fireplace was made out of wet clay pounded down until it was very hard. I did some of the tamping with a board to make this clay harder. This space in front of the fire would be the mother's cooking floor.

The mouth of the fireplace was lined with mudcats made from packing together clay, grass, and water. These large mud packs were pressed into brick-like shapes. The mudcats were sealed onto the wood with mud.

Building the chimney was done very carefully. A boxlike frame of small split logs which had been notched at the corners and pegged to the cabin was constructed. This was fun to watch! These frames extended up about four or five feet. Mudcats were then placed all along the

Chimney base

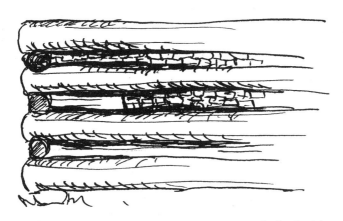

...and chinked logs

interior of this frame and sealed against the wood to make a firebox.

The rest of the chimney was put together with oak sticks. All of the chimney was lined with wet clay. I needed help to carry the water used for chimney lining. Many hands were needed on this day, but everyone was always amazed at what we accomplished.

One of the pioneer's fears was that a chimney would catch on fire. Thus, on cabin-raising day we put a big long pole from a skinny tree outdoors right next to the new mud and stick chimney. Then if rain washed away the mud and the wood caught fire from a spark, the owner could push the flaming chimney away from the cabin.

After the cabin was all assembled, the cracks between the logs needed to be filled by chinking and daubing. Boys like me were able to drive short pieces of wood between the logs, wedging them in by driving one on top of another. This job was called chinking. Then soft clay was daubed or plastered over the chinking both inside and outside. If time allowed us to add a finishing touch, we could drag our fingers along the soft, wet clay. This left a fluted effect when it dried.

The entire family of each neighbor was part of cabin-raising days. The womenfolk again prided themselves in bringing their best foods to share during the noon meal. Friendly talk and offering your talents to a neighbor helped a community to form.

Our Life in the Cabin in the Woods

Mother's Garden

Our family garden was always the responsibility of Mother. She had carefully brought her dried seeds for herbs such as sage and dill from our Franklin County land.

Mother's garden was her pride and joy. Many potatoes, beans, pumpkins, cabbages, and turnips were planted in the rich soil. As other pioneers came, she could trade seeds with them. Soon she had radishes, lettuce, melons, and peas. Roots for rhubarb, horseradish, and asparagus were placed in special garden sections. These delicacies would need protection, since they produce food year after year without replanting.

I can never remember seeing my mother completely idle during the day. She was always busy and occupied with all of the chores that it took to raise a large family of twelve children.

Eventually colorful flowering plants such as marigolds, touch-me-nots, bachelor's buttons, and morning glories grew near our windows or around our doorways.

Tomatoes were believed to be poisonous, so they were grown to bring colorful decorations to our cabin.

Fireplaces and Cooking

The cooking crane hung above the fireplace opening, and it was fitted with three hooks of different lengths so that a pot could be hung high or low over the coals for different heats. The crane could be swung out or in from the fire when you needed to reach the pot.

Corn meal was our staff of life. For several years we had it in some form for breakfast, dinner, and supper. We never got tired of corn meal. We ate a great amount of corn dodger, which was meal mixed with water, salt, and butter. Then it was baked close to the fire in our spider skillet.

Johnnycake was mixed in the same way, but it was baked on a clapboard tilted up before the fire. Hoe cake was the same mixture but was flattened out with the cook's hands and placed on a griddle to bake. Corn meal mush was a big favorite in the early days. Mush and milk was a common meal at supper time. Fried mush with maple syrup and butter made a delicious breakfast. We got along quite well having corn bread for every meal.

Our family ate mostly pork from our hogs and wild game meat. Deer were so plentiful that we ate venison until we were tired of it. We also ate turkeys, squirrels, and pheasants.

Preserving meat required work. To save meat for a

few weeks or months we had to hang it over a bed of coals to half dry and half cook. Then it was hung in a cool place for future use.

Bear meat was eaten occasionally. It was strong in flavor and extra oily.

Fall Creek was full of fish like suckers, cat fish, bass, perch, walleyed pike, and red eye. We speared our fish with a gig as we floated our canoe along in the clear water.

GIG

We kept chickens just to produce eggs. The eggs were so important for baking the corn bread as well as eating fried or scrambled.

The women tended the cows. Milking them twice daily was a woman's chore. Often the woman milked them

in the pasture as the cow ate. A three-legged stool was carried by the milkmaid into the field so that she had a place to sit as she milked. Then the product was used for butter, cottage cheese, and drinking.

Pap always made a good supply of maple sugar. The trees were tapped in the early spring. The pioneer used the same methods as the Indians had used. Then the sap

 was boiled down in a huge kettle over a fire. This lengthy task took days until the graining occurred. This maple syrup was our sugar supply because maple sugar was the only sweetening that we had.

Our simple table had been made by Pap. It held our pewter plates, tin cups, iron spoons, knives, and forks. The forks had just two prongs. We had our ups and downs, but nobody was hungry. Complaining about our home or food was seldom heard. We just lived off the land and were satisfied.

Clothing for Our Family

Our clothing was dependent upon what we could grow or raise safely in the area. Pap didn't have sheep for several years because wolves were a common prey. The deep forests also were full of plant-making burrs, briars, and thick bushes. These would easily stick to the wool of a sheep and make the fleece useless.

Some of the pioneers fashioned britches and hunting shirts from animal skins such as deer. However, Pap and Mother made certain that we wore linen clothing.

Linen cloth was made from the threads of the flax

plant. Every spring we would put out about a half acre of flax, and it would grow much like wheat or grass. In the late summer, when the flax was ripe, the plant was pulled up by the roots and spread on the ground to dry. After the plant seemed dry, it was bundled and stored in the barn until fall. After a few weeks I helped lift it from the barn to open ground outside. The fall rains rotted the inside of the stalk. The outside would stay firm. After the rotting process, the brittle plants were again bound up and put into the barn.

When the harvest of corn was over, we could resume the flax process. In order to get only the linen threads from the plant, I helped use a hand breaker. I would grab a bundle of plants and scrunch them in one hand. By

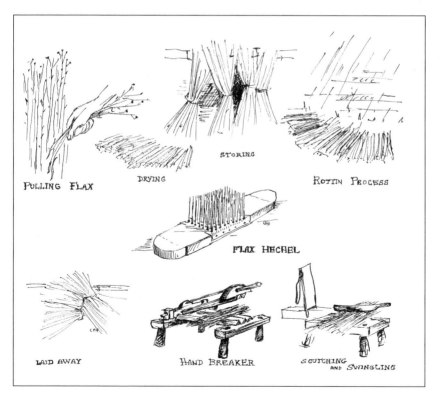

PULLING FLAX   DRYING   STORING   ROTTIN PROCESS

FLAX HECHEL

LAID AWAY   HAND BREAKER   SCUTCHING AND SWINGLING

hacking the plant stems with a wooden knife, the dry heart of the stalk would fall out. The dry outside fiber was left to be drawn through a flax hechel. This board with many sharp iron spikes sticking up would remove the seeds and root ends. As we drew them through a finer flax hechel, the fibers split up into fine silky strands. All of these strands were wrapped around a distaff, and now the flax was ready for spinning.

Louisa, my older sister, learned to spin by the time she was twelve years old. To spin, you stuck one end of the distaff in a hole in the frame of the spinning wheel. The spinner then started the wheel with her foot and with one hand she started the thread by pulling a little from the distaff while the other hand fed the thread in on the reel. The thread was gauged as it passed through her fingers; thus, if it felt too big, it was jerked back to draw the fiber out thinner. If it was too thin, it was given a quick jerk from the distaff to feed more on. The thread was wound on a reel called a skein. Then the skein of thread was boiled in lye to bleach and soften the threads.

The linen thread was now ready for the weaver. For payment we either bartered with the weaver or gave her some money. The linen cloth was made into dresses for the women and girls, and shirts and britches for the men and boys. Underwear was something the men and boys didn't have until we started raising sheep. We wore linen clothing both during the summer and winter, and if you were too cold during the winter, you put on two shirts and two pairs of britches. All cloth that we used was made out of linen. Mother even spun me a fish line made out of linen thread.

When we started raising sheep, the spinning of

Linen spinning wheels like this one were much smaller than woolen wheels.

Woolen spinning wheel

woolen thread was done much the same way as it was for linen. Sometimes mother colored the thread; then we had plaid goods. In these early days about an inch of wool was cut off to get rid of the burrs. Boys and men mostly wore plain, broadrimmed woolen hats. Woolen head coverings were used during the harsh winters.

The first headwear for women was ordinary sunbonnets. Later imported dress goods arrived up from river towns, such as Cincinnati. The women made bonnets of all shapes and colors.

As far as shoes were concerned, they were all made in the evening by Pap. Pap would buy or trade for a half-side of sole leather and a half-side of upper leather. He had brought with him patterns and tools to shape the boots or low moccasins which he diligently crafted. Pap's and Mother's shoes were made first, then shoes for the girls, and finally for the boys. I was the oldest boy; therefore, often I didn't get my shoes until near Christmas time. I often went barefooted on the frosty ground and sometimes even on the ice. On frosty mornings in the fall we would heat a clapboard before the fire-place until it was almost charred, stick it under our arm and run through the frost until our feet began to sting. We would then throw the clapboard down, warm our feet, and make another run until we reached the schoolhouse. We didn't suffer much from the cold or think much about it.

Early Grist Mills

When the pioneers settled a new area, land was first used near a river or a steadily flowing creek. The man who knew how to operate a grist mill bought land next to the rapidly flowing water. Meal made from ground corn or wheat at the grist mill was an essential food for cooking or baking.

Freely flowing water from the White River gave the Whitinger Grist Mill enough power to turn corn or wheat into meal. The usual plan was for the mill to be built on

GRIST MILL

ground that was lower than the waterway. Then the water poured downward with gravity speed into buckets attached to the large water wheel.

The water wheel would run some wooden gears that would in turn run two mill stones. Stonemasons had carved mill stones from boulders found in the area. Each stone had ridges called burrs that rubbed, mashed, and ground the grains for the pioneer's use. The miller would keep a portion of your grain in payment for grinding your grain.

When the weather got really cold and the river froze, the mills had to shut down. This meant that we had to often borrow meal from a neighbor, barter for some of Mr. Whitinger's supply, or eat potatoes.

Since I was the oldest son of our family, I was the child designated to go to the mill. As soon as I was big enough to get upon a horse and ride, I was sent though the frightening woods to get our grist ground at the mill. Corn or wheat had to be ground for your family every two weeks. Freshly ground meal would be mouldy if kept longer.

Always when Pap sent me to the mill, I was filled with fear. What would I do if the horse fell and all of the grain spilled on the ground? Stories of angry Indians who attacked pioneers continued to be told among my neighbors. And then a panther had been recently seen nearby. I never let Pap know how scared I was because I knew there was no choice about going. Our family needed a food supply. So Pap lifted me aboard the horse and placed two bushels of shelled corn on the back of the horse. I left on my journey to Whitinger's Mill.

On one of these trips to the mill my horse got too close to a tree branch. The bag of corn was snagged by the tree. Shelled corn began falling from the hole. I could not get down from the horse in this thicket, so I stuffed one of my gloves in the hole to stop the leaking of the corn.

When I arrived at the mill, I told the miller about my problem. Mr. Whitinger was very understanding; however, I worried about what Pap would do to me after I arrived home. The miller's wife sewed up the hole in the bag. The miller didn't take his portion of the grain, and so by the time I got home, it was a forgotten matter.

Our family had a food supply crisis the second year we lived at our new place. Corn was eaten every day and our harvest had been small. Pap had been so busy clearing land that he didn't get enough planted in the spring.

We had heard that the Conner brothers up the White River had plenty of corn to sell. So Pap borrowed the McCormick's canoe. Neighbors were quick to lend to one another. Pap loaded in his provisions for the long trip up the river. The poles he used to

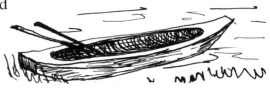

row against the current helped speed him along on the eighteen mile trip.

In order to pay for the corn, Pap was forced to sell his wedding coat to a young man in need. The agreed-upon price was fifteen dollars. When he made the deal with the Conners for one dollar a bushel, Pap was satisfied that the money would feed his family until the next harvest. He also felt he had been taken advantage of by the sellers with the high price.

Pap had to harvest his corn and carry it on his

shoulder to the canoe which was one mile from the field. The trip coming back down the river was much easier. He walked home through the woods, got a horse, and made three or four trips to bring the corn home.

Hunting for Wild Game

The flintlock gun which hung over our fireplace was a symbol of manhood. Pap used this gun to shoot the wild game. This meat was a main food supply for our family.

When I was big enough to load the rifle and shoot it, then I was allowed to hunt. Pap and the other adult pioneers didn't want to waste any lead or powder. So, if I could not shoot the animal in the head, then the rifle stayed home. I became a good, accurate shot because I loved to hunt.

Most every hunter had a name for his gun. Long Barrel was the name Pap gave his rifle. The first thing I learned was the proper procedure for loading the gun. You had to be clever with your hands and fingers as you placed the powder, patchin, and bullet in the barrel of the gun, finally using the ramrod to fix it in place. The flint on the rifle would be struck and that would ignite the powder and the gun would go off.

Water and dampness were a real problem; thus, if either the powder or flint got wet, the gun would not go off.

A hunter always left the cabin with his hunting gear carefully arranged. Hunters were equipped with a shot pouch and a powder horn. The pouch was about six or eight inches square, made from deer hide with the hair left on. It was carried on the right side by a strap running over the left shoulder of the hunter. The powder was fastened to the small strap and hung over the shot pouch. Hunters took lots of pride in their powder horn which was made from a cow or oxen horn, scraped and polished until it was thin and clear. You could even see the powder through it. Up above the powder horn and fastened to the shoulder strap in front was a small scabbard riveted together with lead rivets so as not to dull the edge of the small butcher knife carried in it. Hanging by a short leather thong was the powder charger. This was a measuring cup made from the tip of a deer horn.

The joy of hunting for your family's food gave a boy real pride. Squirrels were easy to kill because they were plentiful. They were also tasty.

I was hunting down along our new ground one time when I saw a flock of turkeys feeding in our corn field. We had shucked the corn, and they were picking around on the ground for the ears we had missed. I slipped up to a fence corner right easy, rested the barrel of the rifle on a fence rail, and just as I drew a bead on a turkey another one walked right in line behind the first one. The bullet killed the front turkey and then went through the back of the other one. I could not wait to go and tell Pap!

Our family never tired of the best and sweetest meat—pheasant or grouse. These birds were not plentiful, so when Pap got one, our meal was treasured.

Pap had a special area of the woods to use for his infrequent deer hunt. The venison, or deer, would last us for some time, so he was careful to use this opportunity only when we had a need for plenty of meat.

Hardly a fall passed when I was a kid without hearing of a bear or two being killed. One of the most exciting times of my youth was a bear chase that started from our cornfield. Mother came in one evening and said that she heard a "breaking and snapping of corn stalks" down in

the cornfield. We heard the cornstalks cracking again the next night and we reported this to Pap, who was ill with ague at the time.

The next day some of us children went down to see what the cornfield looked like. We reported to Pap that the corn had been broken down in little patches, and that something had gone around and taken a bite out of a pumpkin here and there. (Pumpkins were planted in the cornfield too.)

Pap said, "That was a bear that done that, and those patches of corn broken down were where the bear sat down and reached out to pull the stalks to him."

As soon as Pap felt better he sent me to get his brother, Uncle Tom. Uncle Tom came with his rifle named Old Crowbar, and his hound dog, Cump. (This was a name shortened from Tecumseh.) They took Old Cump down in the cornfield and put him on the trail of the bear. The old hound knew his business as he snorted, sniffed, and circled around. Finally he started off almost straight west, his head to the ground. Every once in a while Cump let out a short bay and the men quickly followed.

After an hour or so Old Cump, who had gotten some distance ahead, gave out a long deep bay which meant that he had caught up with the bear and had routed him out of his den. Soon after the hunters heard Old Cump baying like he meant business, the dog went off to the south, headed toward the creek.

Meanwhile, all morning Mother and all of us children had been listening to Old Cump's bays until they died out toward the west. Toward noon she walked to the door again. "Listen, children! I believe I hear Old Cump again and he's headed this way!" said Mother. In fact the bear had turned east at the creek, and Pap and Uncle Tom had cut back as fast as they could, but he had too much start on them. We all lined up with Mother on the post and rail fence in front of the cabin and waited!

The old bear was loping along. He threw his front feet to one side and then to the other. He looked like he was very tired. Old Cump was right behind the bear, baying his

best. Mother raised up on the fence, cupped her hands to her mouth and gave the old hound a long "Whoop-ee-ee!"

The dog surely understood Mother, for he charged right in and seized the bear by the ham. Down went the bear and the dog in a heap, and when the men came up, the bear was reaching out and striking at Old Cump with all of his might. The hound was back out of reach. Both bear and dog then disappeared in the woods, and Old Cump's bays got fainter and fainter in the distance.

Pap and Uncle Tom came trailing along. Both were out of breath. Cump had chased the bear about a mile north of our cabin and the bear went up in a tree, as Mother had predicted. According to hunting rules of those days, Uncle Tom got the first shot at the bear because he was the first to come on the game. Uncle Tom fired. The bear made a few kicks, tumbled out of the fork of the big oak tree, and fell end over end on the ground.

He was so fat that he busted open on the side that he hit. Uncle Tom stayed with the bear while Pap came after the oxen and a cart to haul the dead animal home.

Pap let me go back with him to get the dead bear. We had to cut and slash our way through the woods to get the cart situated so that they could roll the bear aboard. Pap told me to break a switch off and distract the oxen from the bear by switching them and yelling, "Whoa!" If the oxen had gotten a sniff of the bear, they might have just run through the woods. The oxen couldn't stand the looks or smell of a bear, dead or alive! We skinned and dressed the bear. The whole neighborhood had bear meat for a change.

Driving the Hogs to the River

Back in these early times, we drove our hogs to river markets on the Ohio River at places like Cincinnati, Lawrenceburg, and Madison. The reason these markets were so attractive to us was that selling our corn up here in Indianapolis was so bad. The price for corn had gotten down to only ten cents per bushel. This all happened because of the huge supply of corn. The pioneers had cleared land and planted more and more corn each year, and the supply of corn was so much greater than the demand for corn.

CORN

We settlers didn't take long to find out that feeding hogs and driving them to these river markets was a good way to sell our corn. Our family was no different. So we raised hogs and drove them to the river so that they could go on flatboats down to places like Memphis or New Orleans. Most of the hogs we raised were rough looking, long legged, and long snouted. This type of pig could stand the long walk to the Ohio River. Hogs that were plump or rather fat would never make it to the river.

Everybody's hogs ran loose and grew up in the woods in sort of a half-wild state. We would throw out some corn for them each evening to keep them coming up to the barn, and all day they rooted around through the woods eating roots and herbs and anything else they could find. In the fall we drove them to the beech tree thicket. A pond or swamp nearby would provide their needed water. We put out some salt and left them to feed on the beechnuts

for a few weeks. The hogs would then put on some weight pretty fast! Finally, in the fattening-out process, we brought them in and placed them in a rail pen and fed them all the corn they could eat for awhile.

Several farmers would get together for a hog drive to the Ohio River after the hogs, from each farmer, had their ears marked a certain way. A drove of hogs might contain two or three hundred hogs. Big droves handled better than small ones, as the animals would stay together and not scatter. A boss man on a horse was in charge of a drive. Pap got that job almost every time. Six or eight drivers walked on foot to keep the pigs herded. A wagon with four horses and a driver were used to pick up the hogs that could walk no more.

The few roads that led to the Ohio River were more like trails with lots of wagon ruts, and plenty of mud. It took fifteen to twenty days to drive the hogs to Cincinnati. We never took any corn with us, as it would require the use of another wagon. This would not pay. So we bought corn for the customary high price of fifty cents a bushel at all taverns. At night we stayed at taverns along the route. Along towards evening the tavern keeper just ahead would ride out on the path to

find out from the boss how many men to expect, how many hogs, and how much corn to put out in pens for the night feed. On our arrival at the tavern, we drove the hogs into the lot, unloaded the wagon with the tired hogs, put our horses up and fed them, then went to the house and cleaned up as best we could. After a day's drive, we were generally covered with mud from head to foot. We tried to wash ourselves off each evening, but it was difficult. I was nearly always a driver on these drives with Pap. I can tell you we all worked hard, but we rather enjoyed it too.

We washed up and the innkeeper fed us a supper of hot biscuits with honey or maple syrup and a slab of ham. Later we sat around a blazing big fire in the kitchen fireplace, reviewed the day's work, or spun yarns while we dried off. The first day on the drive we went a pretty good distance, but after that it slowed down, as the hogs got tired. The boss got a bed, but most of us drivers would pull off our boots, spread our comforter or blanket on the floor, roll up the carpet for a pillow, and sleep with our feet to the fire in the kitchen of the inn.

After an early breakfast, the boss paid the tavern bill, which was fifty cents a head for the men. The teamster, or the man that drove the wagon, hitched up his horses. We turned out our hogs from the pen and we were on our way once again. When we reached the slaughterhouse near the river, a bargain was struck for the hogs which was anywhere from a dollar and fifty cents to two-fifty a hundred pounds, depending on the quality of the animals. The hogs were weighed alive by catching them by the ears and weighing them on a big steelyard. At this point all of the hogs' earmarks were checked. Then the weights were recorded in the records of the correct farmer-owner. All of the money was kept by the boss until he reached home and settled with the owners.

Once the hogs were slaughtered they were packed and placed in river boats and sent down to New Orleans. This was a good way for the farmers to get money for their corn as they sold it through their hogs.

After a day spent taking in the town and buying goods to take home to the home folks, or to an Indianapolis store on order, we then loaded the wagon with the goods. The drivers needed to walk back to Indianapolis due to the load of goods on the wagon. It only took us five days to walk home and Pap would let us ride his horse part of the way. He would ride up the road, tie his horse, and walk on himself. Then we would take turns riding the horse all day.

Schooling...
and Other Everyday Problems

The Three R's

When I was about seven years old, Pap and some of the neighbors got together and decided to build a schoolhouse and start some education for their youngsters. They held a meeting and elected three men to be trustees, and one of them was Pap. Their job was to build a schoolhouse, hire a teacher, and provide for his board. All questions that came up between the schoolmaster and the patrons of the school were to be settled by  the trustees. Pap offered a plot of ground on our property to set the schoolhouse and it was centrally located for most of the kids that would be going to the school. The men and the big kids of the neighborhood got together and in a few days built a log house without a cent of outlay from anybody.

Inside the schoolhouse the men and big boys built the furnishings. The room was about twenty-by-twenty feet, the door on one side, and opposite the door was the master's chair and table. In one end was a big fireplace, and on the opposite end was a rough board shelf placed on wood pins that stuck out from the log wall. This was called a writing table.

The benches that we sat on were made from slabs split from logs. The legs for the benches were placed on the flat side of the log, leaving the round side up for us to sit on with our short legs. The benches got very tiresome after sitting there a long time. If you wanted to rest your back, you could sort of "hunker down" with your elbows

on your knees and slide back a little to get your feet off the floor. Once in a while a scholar, as we called ourselves, would slide back too far, lose his balance, and flop! There he or she would be on the hard puncheon floor.

We had no desks, and our two books and slate were kept on the floor under our benches. Actually, no one had any certain place to sit, but on cold days the big boys and girls would give the benches nearest the fire to the little ones.

Webster's Spelling Book served for both reading and spelling work. *Pike's Arithmetic*, a slate, and a slate pencil furnished the equipment for a scholar.

Teachers, or schoolmasters, as we called them, were difficult to locate. Nearly all of them were single men who were roving the country but not looking for land or a permanent location, like men with families. Some of them were educated and turned out to be mighty good fellows. There were a few, it appeared, that had failed at everything else and then took up teaching. There was no such thing as a woman teacher. It wasn't a woman's job, any more than milking a cow was a man's job.

The pioneer families had to wait until a schoolmaster came around looking for a job. If the trustees took a notion to him, which they generally did, they told him to draw up his article and go around in the neighborhood and see what signers he could get. If he got enough signers to satisfy himself, he was hired by the trustees. The article usually offered a term of three months: December, January, and February. He got his board and pay; generally fifty cents to seventy cents per scholar. During the term the master boarded around in different homes. Large families with several children in school boarded and roomed the master longer than small families.

The first school house burned down after it had been used for only a short time, possibly due to a careless master. Our second school was held in the home of Master Hawkins, who lived about a mile and a half north of us. Even though it was a long trip through the dense woods, Pap signed up my sister, Louisa, and me.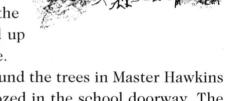

While we played around the trees in Master Hawkins yard at noon hour, he dozed in the school doorway. The first rays of warm spring sunshine lulled him to sleep.

One of the boys noticed a frog hopping close to our sleeping teacher. Soon we were seeing the reason why the frog was moving so quickly. A garter snake had just crawled from under a piece of bark.

Master Hawkins wore buckskin britches that stood out at the bottom. Well, the frog need a hiding place. This scared animal believed that the teacher's open pant leg was a hollow log. Zip! The cold frog was up the britches against Master's warm leg.

Hawkins awoke abruptly, jumped off his bench, and

danced around like a wild man. He failed to hear us telling him what had happened. Slam! Bang! Squeeze!

Mrs. Hawkins heard the clatter and rushed over to see why her husband was yelling and jumping. Quickly she got him into the cabin. He was "got" when he found the lifeless frog. We had a good laugh before he returned to teach the afternoon lessons.

The year after the Hawkins School experiences, we learned some new things. Some families from Pennsylvania and Maryland settled on land on the east side of Fall Creek. These new folks couldn't think of a country without schools for their children, so they started building a schoolhouse right away. Pap, Uncle Ben, and other neighbors quickly helped them. After a new school master

was chosen, school began. I would call this our first organized school. We used the usual books, slates, and other materials such as foolscap paper, quill pens, and ink. Black ink was made by boiling down the bark from a soft maple tree. Red ink was made from boiling pokeberries.

Our school started at six o'clock in the morning. People believed in getting a full day out of the master when they hired him. School would open by the master calling, "Come to books!" We would then rush and scramble for our seats. We could sit anywhere. It didn't make any difference how much noise you made, just so you sat down. We always started the day with our arithmetic lesson. The scholars would be using different pages of the book. Some of us would get pretty well through the book while others never got very far.

Sometimes, about the middle of the forenoon and again in the afternoon, the master would say: "Get your writing lesson." Then we would make a scramble for the writing table. The master had a copy ready for each scholar and he would instruct us on how to hold the pen and how to shape the letters. More attention was given to writing than any other study.

Spelling was the second most important subject. To recite spelling, the scholars, one at a time, were asked how far they had gotten; then the master had you spell and pronounce from the book. The master would take the book and pronounce to you. You spelled. Being a champion or best speller was a coveted honor.

The focus of the reading lesson was upon your ability

to pronounce the words correctly. During reading we got up and read the lesson aloud. Some students could read the whole lesson without a pause. They paid no attention to punctuation. The schoolmaster made corrections only on pronunciation, leaving a word out, or substituting a word. If the master got short of time you might read twice a week. Then again it might be twice a day just according to the teacher's wishes. Comprehending the message of the story wasn't important.

The little ones in the school had their own primer books. Their only work was to learn the ABC's. About the only time they got to recite was when the master got through with the big scholars in time. During recitation the master would point out a letter for the young scholar to name. Little ones recited all the way from once a day to once a week. In most of the early schools, scholars studied out loud, and that made a terrible uproar in the room. I remember one girl whose voice was so loud that you could not think. Therefore, when she opened up, you'd just as well lay your book down.

The early schoolmasters were very strict on some things and they used the gad very often, especially if they were in bad humor. Many masters were not very particular about your lessons or how much you stayed away from school, for they didn't have to bother with you.

The Custom of Turning Out the Master

Every family recognized Christmas in a religious way, but no one gave presents or celebrated Christmas Day. We went to school on Christmas and New Years if they fell on a week day, just the same as any other day.

In all of the county schools it was a custom for the

master to treat his scholars with apples and ginger cakes. Then while the children ate they could break away from the lessons.

Sometimes a master had no treat ready for Christmas Day. He may have made no preparation or he could just have decided to refuse to buy a treat. If the scholars sensed no treat was going to be received, the students locked the master out of the school on the special day. The teacher would be kept out until he agreed upon a treat. The parents and the trustees of the school agreed with the students on this special plan. Usually the masters we had were ready on Christmas morning with their treat, and we spent the day eating apples and ginger cakes. We also played games and had a jolly good time!

For several years all of the masters did the treating very well, but one year the trustees had trouble finding a master. None had shown up in the neighborhood looking for a job so our folks had to get one of those Marylanders that had moved in east of us. His name was Mr. Brown. Mr. Brown was a good master and we all liked him. Everything went along well until Christmas. We scholars didn't say anything to him about a treat. We thought that he was such a good man so we never doubted that he would be on time with the apples and ginger cakes.

On Christmas Day, as was our custom, we arrived at the schoolhouse very early in anticipation of the treat. The students barred the door and waited for his arrival. That day one of his sons showed up instead of Mr. Brown. No doubt word had gotten out about the plan of the students.

We told the young Brown boy to go back and tell his pap that the door was locked until the master brought a treat. When his son reported back, Mr. Brown flew into a rage. He shook his fists and said that no mob could keep him out of his schoolhouse.

Mrs. Brown came running down to Uncle Ben's house and told Uncle Ben that her husband was carrying on something awful. He was swearing like a sailor, which was not his normal behavior. Uncle Ben then went over and talked to Mr. Brown. My uncle told the master how things were done here in Indiana. Mr. Brown was informed that all he had to do was take a little treat to school, give the youngsters time to eat the treat, and all would be well.

Mr. Brown never came on Christmas Day. But the next day he was on hand, pleasant as you please, with apples, ginger cakes, and a jug or two of spruce beer. This was a drink commonly made by these German settlers from the East. We had a fine day of it after all. Mr. Brown held no grudge. He seemed to enjoy himself as much as any of us.

On another Christmas Day, a master named Lynch didn't treat either. He left the neighborhood completely, never to be seen again. Thus, our school was over for the year.

Then there was Mr. Gill, a master that everyone liked. But he didn't want to treat either. We locked him out and we finally tied him up and laid him in the middle of the road where a hog drive was coming through on its way to the  Ohio River. Some of these hogs were rough-looking, long-tusked, and half-wild boars. One of these boars came up really close to Mr. Gill. The animal started pawing the ground, sniffing and chomping his jaws like he was going to jump right on him.

That was more than Mr. Gill could stand. He agreed to give us a treat. The next day Master Gill gave us one of the finest treats we ever had.

These were some of the practices and customs of the early schools in Indiana.

Ills and Aches

Sickness in the early days was different from how it is now. The country was new and we lived far from our neighbors. We ate plain food, and we spent most of our time out in the fresh air. The few doctors that were in the new state didn't know what to do with us when we got sick. In many cases, if a person didn't have the body or the backbone to whip a sickness, then he or she just didn't pull through. People died, and nobody knew what was the matter with them. A lot of families did home medicine and women used remedies their mothers had taught them.

Malaria or ague, as we called it, was the most common complaint among the settlers. Most everyone had a spell of it in the fall. The settlers tried to shape up their work in the late summer before they got down with the chills. These were symptoms of ague. If ague couldn't be broken in its early stages, it would last for several months. We thought it was caused by the dense, damp woods, and the rotten logs and leaves.

Home remedies were used to get rid of ague. One such remedy was a tea made from a herb called boneset.

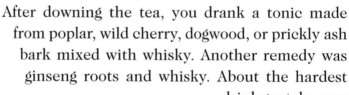

After downing the tea, you drank a tonic made from poplar, wild cherry, dogwood, or prickly ash bark mixed with whisky. Another remedy was ginseng roots and whisky. About the hardest drink to take was made from gun barrel water. First you fired a rifle until the barrel was black from burnt powder. Then you filled the barrel with water to stand overnight. The suffering person then drank the water.

Children's complaints were doctored with teas made from spicewood, sassafras bark, or peppermint leaves.

As new settlers came to our area, we were able to learn new remedies. Calomel was one of the store remedies used often by the first doctors. Another product was called "Thunder and Lightning," and it was a shock to use. Then came Sappington's Pills, which became a universal remedy for ague.

Most of the doctors believed in bleeding in the early days. First thing they would do is have you roll up your sleeve. Then you had to grab a broom handle to extend your arm veins. Then the doctor would proceed with the operation. After a certain amount of blood dripped from your body, your cut was bandaged to stop the flow. You were then expected to feel better soon.

Accidents, like cuts and broken bones, were usually taken care of at home. I remember when one of my younger brothers fell and broke his arm. Pap carried him to the house and examined his arm. Pap then whittled out some thin poplar splints. He bound these to the broken arm. It wasn't long until his arm was as good as ever.

One time, I slashed my shin with an adz, which made a nasty looking cut. Soon it started to swell. Mother was worried. A traveler stopped by our house. He said he could heal my leg if we would bring him a basket of beech leaves. He then placed the leaves in a pot and boiled them for an hour or so. Eventually he put a poultice around my leg with the boiled leaves. In a day or so the swelling went down and my leg started to heal and it got all right. It

might be my leg was ready to heal anyhow, but people had much faith in their remedies, and I suppose that helped us some too.

We didn't know much about dentists back then. If you had a toothache, you either grinned and beared it, or you hunted up a doctor. He would pull the tooth. If no doctor was handy, and the tooth ached badly, then you would apply to a blacksmith. He would knock the tooth out with a punch.

Due to many illnesses, people got to be old looking when they were very young. Raising big families brought the woman down very fast. The men generally outlived their wives. The exposure and hardship or frontier life, along with the lack of knowing what to do for sicknesses, no doubt shortened many a life.

After This Story . . .

New families continued to move to Indianapolis during Ollie's youth. One day in 1839 he saw a beautiful girl in a canoe. Pamelia Howland and her family were settled on land across Fall Creek from the Johnson homestead. The Howlands had come from Saratoga Springs, New York, to Indiana. Even though her family brought new ways of living to the area, she and Oliver courted and eventually were married. The very well-known preacher, Henry Ward Beecher, performed the ceremony in 1843. Oliver farmed for Pamelia's father until Oliver could buy his own land.

To the marriage of Oliver and Pamelia were born four children: Silas, who became a prominent farmer near Millersville; Frank, who farmed at the corner of Thirty-eighth Street and Fall Creek Boulevard; Mary; and James. The latter two children spent their adult lives in Terre Haute, Indiana. Since this was far from Indianapolis in the late 1800s, their stories aren't known.

Oliver and Pamelia's son, Frank, had a farm located directly across Thirty-eighth Street from Oliver's childhood homeplace. In 1873 Frank and his wife, Georgia Pursel Johnson, were blessed with a son, Howard, the young man who wrote down his grandfather's stories on a school tablet. Later they had a second son, William.

Oliver was then fifty-two years old. He set about giving his grandchildren stories and skills needed for a good farm life. When Howard and Bill were youngsters, Grandfather Oliver made almost anything they wanted to play with on the farm. Grandpa could make the best wagons and sleds you ever saw. He made bows and arrows that would kill squirrels and rabbits. Oliver showed the boys how to make Indian suits and moccasins, how to trap, skin, and tan hides, and how to make fringe for hunting shirts and leggings. Sometimes Grandpa would use his big hand to rub away almost any pain or ache; especially pains associated with green apple time! Oliver also took his grandsons on hunting and fishing trips. He was an excellent carpenter. He allowed his grandchildren to use his tools and helped them make things in his shop. Howard thought Grandpa was the most wonderful man in the world.

When Oliver grew too old to operate his farm, Howard, now married to Minnie Fessler Johnson, moved into the large house with Oliver and Pamelia. This structure still stands on North Park Avenue near Forty-sixth Street in Indianapolis, Indiana. Oliver's former farm is known as the Johnson Woods Addition to the local residents today.

The two men spent winter evenings going over the old stories of Oliver's days in the "new" Indianapolis. Now

Howard's zeal to remember this oral history became real. He carefully wrote the recollections on school tablets.

In 1951, through encouragement of a cousin, Howard shared these materials with the Indiana Historical Society. A book, *Home in the Woods*, written by Howard Johnson, is an authentic collection of early times in the new state. Later the same material was published by the Indiana University Press in the 1970s.

Howard and his wife, Minnie, eventually moved to a new farm located where Seventy-ninth Street and Ditch Road now are. Children, Franklin and Alice, were born to this couple. Oliver died in 1907, the year of Alice's birth. The stories given now orally by Howard to Alice, her husband, Thomas Hessong, and their children, Robert and Carolyn, continued to affirm that the generations beyond Oliver would learn of the wonders of the new land. Creating Indianapolis was truly a story to be remembered and told over and over.

Howard became the wonderful grandfather to Robert Hessong and Carolyn Hessong Hickman by using his own dear Grandpa as a model. Since these families often lived in multiple generation homes, Bob had ample time to learn fishing and woodworking from his "Ampie." Carolyn was encouraged as a student and an artist by Howard. Both the author of this book, Bob, and the illustrator, Carolyn, remember the enjoyment of having Ampie help them raise a baby crow that Bob brought to the farmhouse from the woods. Joe, the crow, became a family pet for several years.

Ampie, Bob, cousin Bill Johnson, and Tom Wonell, a neighbor, built a log cabin in the family's farm woods. The woodsmen built this cabin from logs in the late 1940s.

They used tools and techniques very much like the Johnson ancestors had done back in Ollie's time. It was eighteen by twenty feet, and it had a nice fieldstone fireplace. The cabin was used for family gatherings at first. As Indianapolis grew and the farm was sold for tracts to use for homes, the cabin was moved three different times. It now resides attached to Bob's home where he uses it for family, church, and other gatherings.

Currently, fourth grade classes studying Indiana History come through for a brief presentation on pioneer life, then they go to Bob's blacksmith shop where he operates the forge and bellows. The class watches Bob, the blacksmith, make an item for their classroom.

Bob operates the blacksmith shop to imitate his ancestor, Jeremiah Johnson, who was also a smith and the grandfather of Ollie. Finally, the classes are led to the Fall Creek Cemetery in nearby Millersville to visit the cemetery where Oliver, Pamelia, John, and Sarah Johnson are buried. Thus, early Indiana pioneer history continues to be told and remembered.